DATE DUE

JA 29 '11			
MR 05 '11			
NO 30 '10			
DE 08 '16			
AG 30 '18			

Casey and Bella

GO TO
NEW YORK CITY

Written by Jane Lovascio
Illustrated by Aija Jasuna

Publishers Cataloging-in-Publication Data

Lovascio, Jane.
    Casey and Bella go to New York City / written by Jane Lovascio ;
illustrated by Aija Jasuna.
      p. cm.
    Summary: Two dogs spend a day exploring New York City. Along
the way, they make a few new friends and teach them some lessons
in good manners.
    ISBN-13: 978-1-60131-007-1
    [1. Dogs—Juvenile fiction. 2. New York (N.Y.)—Juvenile fiction.
3. Friendship—Juvenile fiction. 4. Manners and customs—Juvenile
fiction. 5. Stories in rhyme.] I. Jasuna, Aija, ill. II. Title.

115 Bluebill Drive
Savannah, GA 31419

Visit our website at www.BigTentBooks.com

Printed and bound in the United States of America

First printing 2007

13 Digit ISBN: 978-1-60131-007-1

Published with the assistance of Dragonpencil.com

This book is dedicated to two furry friends,

Mollie and Bugles,

who brought smiles to the faces of children and adults everywhere.

In honor of her furry friends, the author will make a $2 donation to Loving Paws Assistance Dogs™ for every copy of **Casey and Bella go to New York City** sold through www.CaseyAndBella.com

Loving Paws
Assistance Dogs™

..Special dogs for special kids..

Children and Dogs Working Together
to Achieve Greater Independence

Founded in 1993, Loving Paws Assistance Dogs™ is a non-profit organization that trains dogs to assist children nationwide who are physically disabled. While the majority of Loving Paws placements are with children with spinal cord injuries, Loving Paws also provides Service and Social Dogs to children with Muscular Dystrophy, Cerebral Palsy, Spina Bifida, and other disabilities. Loving Paws is a fully accredited voting member of Assistance Dogs International.

To learn more visit: www.lovingpaws.com

Casey walked the window sill and pressed her nose against the glass.
She whispered to the city beyond the hill, "I hope my owners get home fast."

The door to the apartment opened and
in rushed Jane and Jeff.
"Casey, we are home!" they cried.
"It's like we never left."
She ran right to her owners
to give them both kisses,
first one to the mister,
then more to the misses.

She then sat down by her owners' feet.
They patted her head and gave her a treat.
"We have a surprise for you, Casey," said Jeff.
"There's someone we'd like you to meet."
        "We got another puppy," said Jane,
"from the shelter down the street."

Jeff said, "Casey, this is Bella," as they each gave warm hellos.
Casey sniffed at Bella's snout then Bella licked her nose.
Jeff and Jane were happy that their dogs were friends so soon.
The pair of pets romped and ran the entire afternoon.

Next morning after Jane and Jeff
    left early for their day,
Bella woke up Casey,
    "Come on, let's go outside and play!"
Casey rubbed her eyes and said,
    "There are rules for dogs like us.
Number 1, obey our owners
    without a lot of fuss.

We give lots and lots of kisses,
    that's rule number 2.
And number 3, while in the house,
    we never pee or poo."
"Well," asked Bella,
    "where do we go when we go?"
Casey answered, "We go outside,
    on the grass or the snow."

"Ok, great!" exclaimed Bella.
　　"Let's go right now!"
She tried to open the door
　　but she didn't know how.
Casey shook her head slowly
　　and silently thought,

If we sneak out the door
　　I'm afraid we'll get caught.
But if we can get back
　　before Jane and Jeff do,
we can sneak back inside
　　and they won't have a clue!

"Here we go!" Casey cried
　　as she leapt from the rug.
She grabbed the door handle
　　and gave it a tug.
"Good job!" cheered Bella
　　as the door swung open
and the two dogs ran out
　　into the streets of Hoboken.

Outside, Bella was amazed at what she saw --
grass and trees and flowers galore.
"Wow!" Bella exclaimed "This is great, I must say!
And what are those tall buildings way far away?"
"That's New York City, the Big Apple it's called."
"Let's go there!" said Bella. "Come on,
I'm enthralled!"

"Well, ok, but first we have to get there all the way from Hoboken.
We can take the bus, or the ferry, or hop the train with a token."
They decided on the ferryboat and made it there fast.
They were far away from their home before much time had passed.

"Where should we go first?" asked Bella with a bark.
"The greenest place in all New York. They call it Central Park.
First we'll walk through Greenwich Village, and then through old Times Square.
When you see the big oak trees, you'll know we're finally there."

Along the way, Bella asked,
　　"Casey, what is that?
I know it's not a dog
　　and I'm sure it's not a cat."
"That's a squirrel," said Casey.
　　"They are smart and like to run."
So Bella asked the squirrel
　　if he'd like to join their fun.

"I'm busy hiding nuts," said the squirrel scratching his head.
"You can find more nuts in Central Park," little Bella said.
"But me?" said the squirrel. "Me play with you?
You'll just chase me around like other dogs do."
Casey explained, "We're not like that – we're nice.
Bella and I are friends to cats, squirrels, and even mice."

Mister squirrel joined the dogs on their journey to the park.
But on their way there, they were halted by a bark.
A little grey dog, fresh and clean from the spa,
Was yapping at them; a high-pitched Chihuahua.
"What are you doing in Chelsea? This is my neighborhood!
Go back where you came from. Is that understood?"
Casey looked at the Chihuahua and asked, "Can't we share this nice place?"
"I suppose," said the Chihuahua, "there might be enough space.
I'm sorry I barked. There's no need for a fight.
It's important to share. It's fair and it's right."
Casey smiled at the Chihuahua and said, "See you around –
Or would you like to wander with us through downtown?"
"I'd love to come," said the Chihuahua, "Please call me Lance.
You are kind and I thank you for this second chance."

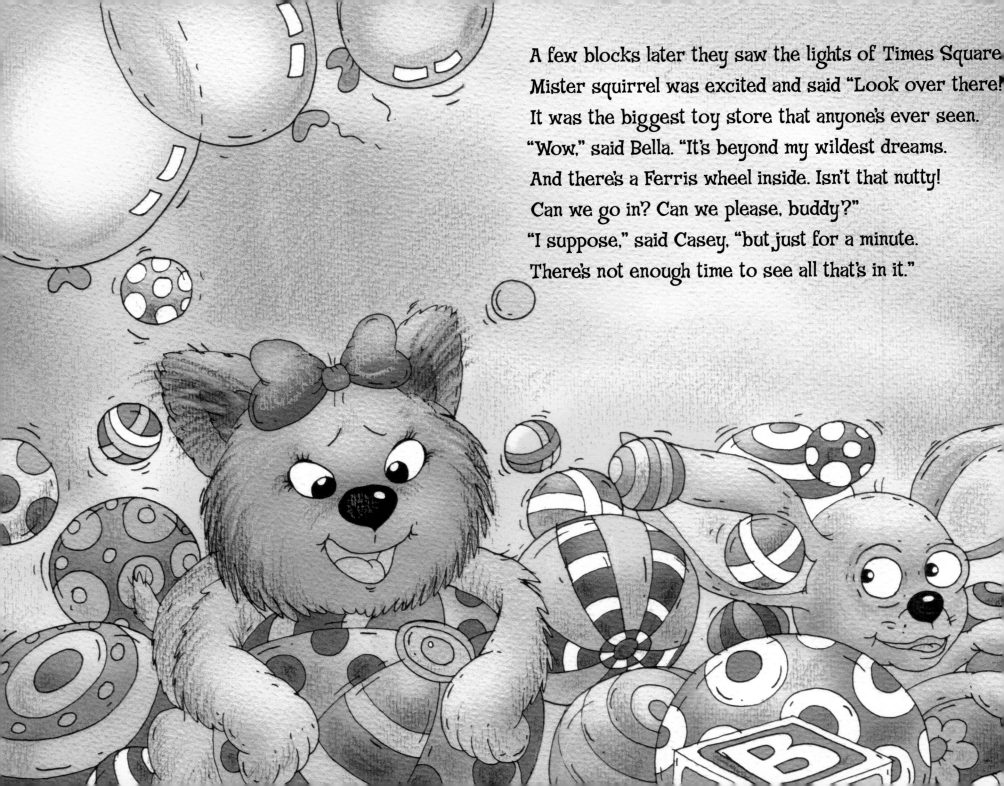

A few blocks later they saw the lights of Times Square
Mister squirrel was excited and said "Look over there!
It was the biggest toy store that anyone's ever seen.
"Wow," said Bella. "It's beyond my wildest dreams.
And there's a Ferris wheel inside. Isn't that nutty!
Can we go in? Can we please, buddy?"
"I suppose," said Casey, "but just for a minute.
There's not enough time to see all that's in it."

The squirrel and three dogs ran all through the store.
There were bicycles, board games, candy, and more!
There were more toys than Bella could ever imagine.
Teddy bears, doll houses, and a little red wagon.
Casey was worried about getting home before dark,
"Look, let's get on our way. It is still ten blocks to the park."

They arrived at the park
      and admired the view,
There were horse-drawn carriages
      and picnics for two.
Bella stared at all of the
      things that were new,
As they walked all the way
      to the Central Park Zoo.
"What is a zebra," asked Bella,
      "and what's a polar bear?"
"They are animals like us," said Casey,
      "and it's not polite to stare."

"Pardon moi," said a poodle, "excuse me!
Please step away or I may catch a flea!"
"That's not nice," said Casey. "We are just as clean as you.
You are no better than us or any animal in this zoo."
"I think not! I live on Central Park West.
I wear a diamond collar and always smell my best."
Casey said, "It doesn't matter where you live or what you wear,"
"What makes you a good friend is being generous and fair."

"I never thought about it that way," said the poodle.
"and I'm sorry I was rude.
Sometimes living in New York
can give you an attitude."
"My name is Muffy," said the poodle,
as she held her head up proud.
"It's nice to meet you," said the squirrel
as he introduced the crowd.

So Muffy took her new friends
        for a hotdog, chips, and water,
and promised never to forget
        the lesson they had taught her.
This was the same lesson Casey taught
        to everyone she greeted –
'treat everyone you meet
        the same as you want to be treated.'

Casey nudged Bella, "It is starting to get dark.
We need to say goodbye and head out from the park.
If we hurry we can get home in time for Jane and Jeff.
They won't suspect for a moment that we ever left."
"Goodbye, everyone! We had fun!" Bella said,
As she and Casey ran off ahead.
They jumped on the train without even a token,
and soon arrived back in good old Hoboken.

They snuck back in, through their open door,
and lay back down on the kitchen floor.
Bella smiled, "That was fun."
"Shhhh," said Casey, "here they come."
"Girls, we are home," shouted Jeff. "It's seven-thirty!"
"Wait a minute," said Jane, "why are your paws so dirty?"

The End

"In order to make a difference
you have to start by not being indifferent."

— *Jane Lovascio*

Jane is a graduate of Boston University with a Bachelor's Degree in Psychology and a background in elementary education. She lives just outside New York City with her husband Jeff and works as a medical sales representative. Jane was inspired to write her story because of her love for children and her two dogs, Casey and Bella. Jane hopes her story will bring happiness to the lives of children as well as to help those with degenerative diseases.